INVASION FROM THE PLANET OF THE COWS

Don't miss these other nail-biting *MAXimum Boy* adventures:

THE HIJACKING OF MANHATTAN

THE DAY EVERYTHING TASTED LIKE BROCCOLI

SUPERHERO . . . OR SUPER THIEF?

starring in
INVASION FROM THE PLANET
OF THE COWS

BY DAN GREENBURG
ILLUSTRATIONS BY GREG SWEARINGEN

A Little Apple Paperback

SCHOLASTIC INC.
New York   Toronto   London   Auckland   Sydney
Mexico City   New Delhi   Hong Kong   Buenos Aires

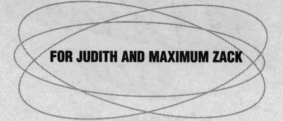

FOR JUDITH AND MAXIMUM ZACK

ISBN 0-439-21947-7

Text copyright © 2001 by Dan Greenburg.
Illustrations copyright © 2001 by Scholastic Inc.

All rights reserved. Published by Scholastic Inc.

SCHOLASTIC, LITTLE APPLE PAPERBACKS, and associated logos are trademarks and/or registered trademarks of Scholastic Inc.

12 11 10 9 8 7 6 5 4 3 2 1   1 2 3 4 5 6 7/0

Printed in the U.S.A.
First Scholastic printing, November 2001

CHAPTER 1

"You'll never guess where *I'm* going today, Max," said my stupid teenage sister, Tiffany.

"OK," I said, "I'll never guess." I was eating breakfast and doing my homework at the same time. I didn't have time to play stupid games with Tiffany.

"No, I meant *try* to guess. Where's the

first place my class is stopping on our field trip to Washington, D.C., this week?"

"Patagonia," I said.

Tiffany stuck out her tongue at me.

"Mom, Max is being a dork," she said. "*You* guess where our first stop is."

"I don't know, dear," said my mom. "Where is your first stop?"

"The place where *Minimum* Boy here got his powers."

"You're going to the Air and Space Museum?" I asked.

Tiffany nodded.

My name is Max Silver. I live in Chicago. I'm eleven years old. I wear glasses and braces. Three years ago, I accidentally handled some rocks in the Air and Space Museum that had just come back from outer space. Right after that I found I could do things most eleven-year-olds can't. Like fly. And lift buses over my head with one hand. If I don't use my superpowers, I'm the second worst athlete in my grade. But if I used them I'd blow my cover, and that would put my family in danger. You probably think I could use just a *little* of my superpowers and be just a *little* stronger and faster than other kids, but that's not how superpowers work. With superpowers it's all or nothing. I hate that.

I have a few weaknesses. I'm allergic to milk products, sweet potatoes, ragweed, and math. Even seeing or hearing a math problem makes me weak and dizzy. Superman had the same problem with kryptonite. I'm the only kid in the sixth grade with a doctor's excuse to get out of math.

The President of the United States

sends me on lots of missions because of my superpowers. Like the time an evil scientist named Dr. Zirkon hijacked the island of Manhattan and towed it out to sea. Or the time a supervillain named the Tastemaker made everything in the country taste like steamed broccoli. Or the time a supervillain called Ethelred the Unready stopped the world and stole the greatest treasures in three countries. My superpowers helped me solve all those crimes.

"So where does the museum keep those space rocks you handled?" Tiffany asked.

"Why do you want to know?" I said.

"I want to see what turned my dorky baby brother into a pooper-hero."

Just then the phone rang. Mom answered it.

"Max, it's the President of the United

States," she said. She handed me the receiver.

"Why is the President always calling Max?" said Tiffany. "He's getting to be such a *pest*."

"Sssshh! Tiffany!" hissed my mother.

"Good morning, sir," I said into the phone.

"Good morning, Max," said the President. "I know you're just about to leave for school, but something has just come up that I need to talk to you about."

"What's that, sir?" I said. Whenever the President says he needs to talk to me, it usually means he's going to send me out on another mission. I've missed so much school because of presidential missions, my homeroom teacher makes me study with a tutor on weekends. I hate that.

"Max, what I have to tell you now is a military secret. Are you speaking on a secure phone?"

"Well, sir, I don't think phones have feelings, so I don't know if this one feels secure or *in*secure."

"I meant is the phone in a place where you can be overheard by agents of a hostile government?"

"Not unless somebody in my family is a spy," I said. "Which I pretty much doubt."

"Good," said the President. "Max, as you know, there are no such things as UFO's. The several thousand UFO sightings we get every month can all be explained as weather balloons or hubcaps falling off airplanes. But it seems that a kind of *non*-UFO has just landed. I'm not at liberty to say where.

But I need you to come to Washington immediately for a top secret briefing."

"How soon is immediately, sir?" I asked. "I'm right in the middle of chewing a piece of toast."

"Swallow it on the way to Washington," said the President.

CHAPTER 2

As soon as I hung up, I put on my Maximum Boy uniform and went to the door.

"Oh, no," said Tiffany. "Not another presidential mission. What is it *this* time? Has somebody hijacked New Jersey?"

"I can't tell you," I said. "It's a military secret."

"Oh, give me a break, Max. Who am *I* going to tell?"

"Tiffany, the President says I can't tell anybody, OK? Mom, Dad, I'm going."

"When will you be home, son?" asked my dad.

"I don't know," I said.

"Max," said Tiffany, "since we're both going to be in Washington today, maybe I could come to the White House and you could introduce me to the President?"

"I'm sorry. We're going to be too busy with matters of national security."

She scroonched up her face and mimicked me, "I'm *sorry*. We're going to be too *bu*sy with matters of *na*-tion-al se-*cur*-i-ty."

"I sure wish you weren't so jealous of my missions," I said.

"Jealous? Jealous of an eleven-year-old dork who wears glasses and braces and faints when he sees a math problem? I am so *not* jealous," said Tiffany. "Dad, am I jealous of Max?"

"Maybe a little," said Dad.

"I don't *faint* when I see a math problem," I said.

"No?" said Tiffany. "Then what would you call it?"

"I just get a little . . . dizzy is all."

"You faint," said Tiffany. "Only wusses faint."

"Oh, yeah? And I suppose wusses kick the butts of supervillains like Dr. Zirkon and the Tastemaker and Ethelred the Unready?"

"Those are such wussy archvillains," said Tiffany. "Anybody could kick those guys' butts."

"Ha!" I said. "I'd like to see *you* do it." I opened the door.

Tiffany got this really evil gleam in her eye.

"Max," she said, "Joe is three-fourths the age of Ben. Ben is two-thirds the age of Jim. If Ben is twelve, how old are Joe and Jim?"

Suddenly, everything got blurry. I fell down in the doorway.

"Tiffany Silver, you go to your room!" yelled my dad. "You know we don't talk math in front of Max."

"OK, OK, I'm sorry," said Tiffany.

"To your room," said Dad. "*Now.*"

"Max, dear," said Mom, helping me up. "Are you all right?"

"Yeah," I said. "I'll get you for this, Tiffany! Not today, maybe not tomorrow, but when you least expect it!"

* * *

When I landed on the White House lawn, two Marines with rifles and white hats ran up to me. They weren't any of the ones I knew.

"This is restricted government property," said one. He pointed his rifle at me. "What are you doing here?"

"The President asked me to get here as soon as possible," I said. "I'm Maximum Boy."

"Oh, Maximum Boy, of course. I've heard of you, sir," said the other Marine. He turned to the one who had asked what I was doing there. "He's a superhero," he said.

"Sorry, sir," said the one who asked what I was doing there. They both saluted me.

The White House Marines salute me a lot, but I still get a kick out of it. I went in-

side and walked to the Oval Office. When I got there, the President was talking with two guys. One was a man in a black suit with a white crew cut. He was J. Edgar Poopington, the head of the FBI. He was also talking to a four-star general I hadn't met.

"Oh, here's Maximum Boy now," said the President. "Good morning, son. Thanks for coming. I think you know Director Poopington. This is General Hurling of the Air Force Strategic Air Command."

"Why, he's just a dadburned kid," said General Hurling in a southern accent. "How old are you, son?"

"Eleven," I said.

"Eleven!" said the general. "Heck, I got *underwear* older than you."

"In spite of his age, Maximum Boy has

handled some pretty tricky situations for us, General," said the President. "I suggest we give him the respect he deserves. Tell him what's going on."

"Oh, all right," said the general. "Son, we have a situation. It seems that a device of unknown origin has landed on a farm in Iowa."

"A UFO?" I asked.

The President, Director Poopington, and General Hurling frowned at me.

"There are no such things as UFO's," said General Hurling. "We get thousands of UFO sightings every month, but the dadburned things always turn out to be either weather balloons or hubcaps falling off airplanes."

"Whatever you say, sir."

"Now then," said General Hurling, "this . . . whatever-it-is has crash-landed in a farm field right outside Cedar Rabbits, Iowa."

"Cedar Rabbits?" I said. "Are you sure you don't mean Cedar *Rapids*?"

"The briefing I got said it was Cedar *Rabbits*," said General Hurling. "Anyway, we got this thing surrounded. So far nobody has come out of the dadburned thing, but if something does, I'd like you to be the first to talk to it."

"Why me?"

"Well, son, because if the dadburned thing proves to be hostile, I want somebody in there with superpowers."

CHAPTER 3

The flying directions General Hurling gave me were pretty good. It took me only about ten minutes to get to Cedar Rapids. The farms below me looked like little squares of green and brown on a patchwork quilt. I flew lower and scanned the fields. And then I saw it. The UFO.

It didn't look anything like what I'd heard a UFO was supposed to look like. It

was silver-colored, but it wasn't shaped like a saucer or a disk. What it was shaped like, at least the way it looked from the air, was a barn. It was surrounded by soldiers. Soldiers with bazookas. Soldiers in tanks. There must have been a hundred of them, all with their guns trained on this silver, barn-shaped UFO.

I swooped down and made a perfect landing in front of a soldier who looked like he might be in charge. He wore sergeant's stripes on his sleeves.

"Sergeant, I'm Maximum Boy," I said. "General Hurling said he'd call to tell you I was coming."

The sergeant saluted me.

"*Sir*, yes *sir*," said the sergeant, "we've been expecting you, sir."

"Good," I said. "Tell me everything that's happened so far."

"Everything, sir?"

"Everything," I said.

"Sir," said the sergeant, "a sound like mooing was definitely heard from the object. Shortly after that, sir, we sent out for pizza.

Half sausage, half pepperoni. Then I had to go to the Porta Potti, sir, and when I got there I found there was no more toilet paper, so . . ."

"OK, OK," I said. "You don't have to tell me *everything*."

"Sir," said the sergeant, "the men want to know — are you going to approach the object and investigate?"

"I might," I said. "I might not."

"If you did approach the object, sir, the men would be very grateful. None of *us* wants to do it."

To tell you the truth, I didn't particularly want to do it, either. But I kind of felt it was expected of me. And I didn't want any more remarks from General Hurling about having underwear older than me.

I nervously approached the UFO. I took

a deep breath. I knocked on the side. I don't know what I expected to happen. Have a slimy green monster from outer space with long tentacles attack me? Have my body suddenly turn to warm red Jell-O? Get sucked into the UFO and eaten by giant black spiders? Nothing happened. I knocked again. Suddenly, a panel slid open.

In the opening stood a cow. A cow in a silver space suit with a clear glass bubble over her head. She didn't look too scary. In fact, she looked kind of silly. I saw the soldiers raise their guns. I was pretty sure they were going to shoot her.

"Hold your fire!" I shouted to the soldiers. Then I turned back to the alien cow.

"Greetings, alien creature," I said nervously. "The people of Iowa and Earth welcome you. We hope you come in peace."

"You speak Cow!" said the alien creature. "How is it that one who is but a calf can speak the language of the cows?"

"Actually, I'm speaking English," I said. "I guess English must be pretty similar to Cow. What's your name?"

"I am General Bossy, Supreme Commander of the Army of the Planet of the Cows. How are *you* called?"

"I am Maximum Boy of planet Earth. Do you come in peace?"

"Well," she answered, "that depends. How are you defining the word 'peace'?"

"Are you here to find out about our culture?" I asked. "Or are you here to kill off the entire population of Earth with death rays?"

"Um, pretty much the first one," said Bossy.

"Sir!" shouted the sergeant. "You want us to start shooting now or what?"

"No, no, hold your fire!" I yelled. "They are cows, and they come in peace!"

"OK, sir!" shouted the sergeant.

I heard rustling as the soldiers lowered their guns.

"So tell me," I said. "Where is the Planet of the Cows?"

"It's in the Milky Way," said Bossy. "Please settle a bet: Is Planet Hollywood a moon of planet Earth?"

"No, Planet Hollywood is a chain of restaurants," I answered. "General Bossy, why have you come to planet Earth?"

"Our continuing mission is to explore strange new worlds. To seek out new life and new civilizations. To boldly go where no cow has ever gone before."

"That sounds a lot like a TV program we have here called *Star Trek*," I said.

"Yes, we are all great fans of *Star Trek* on the Planet of the Cows," she said. "But mainly, we come to planet Earth to check up on colonies of cows that we left here several thousand Earth years ago. We are worried about their safety. Do you know of such colonies of cows?"

"Uh, sure."

"And do they live well?"

"Mm-hmm."

"Tell me," said Bossy. "Do cows have jobs of much responsibility in the government of planet Earth?"

"Uh, well, probably some do," I said. "They have more jobs on farms, though."

"I hope they are well paid for their farm labor," she said.

"You'd have to ask them," I said.

General Bossy took a container of something out of the pocket of her space suit and handed it to me.

"Please accept this token of our friendship," she said. "A glass of healthful and delicious milk. You may drink it now."

"Uh, I can't do that, General Bossy," I said. "I'm really sorry, but I happen to be really allergic to milk products. They make me sick."

Bossy was suddenly furious.

"You refuse to drink our milk?" she shrieked. "You have insulted the entire Planet of the Cows! On our planet such insults are punishable by death! Bork! Come out here immediately!"

There was a terrible noise inside the UFO. Then out clanked a huge steel robot in the shape of a cow.

"Bork," said Bossy, "the milk has been refused!"

A ray came out of the middle of the robot cow's head. It poked around, then landed on a bazooka being held by one of the soldiers. The ray melted the bazooka. The soldier screamed and dropped it. The soldiers behind me aimed their guns again.

"I'm drinking the milk, I'm drinking the milk!" I shouted.

I drank the milk. Bossy and the robot cow calmed down.

"Tell me, is the milk not delicious?" Bossy asked in a normal tone of voice.

"Very delicious, General," I said. I wondered how long it would be before I got sick.

"So," said Bossy. "We have so much to ask you. So very much to learn about your strange civilization. We have heard certain words on TV that we do not understand. What is a cowboy — half cow and half boy?"

"No, a cowboy is a man who, uh, sees to it that cows get from one place to the other."

"Oh," said Bossy. "Like a tour leader?"

"A little like a tour leader, yeah," I said.

"And what is a sacred cow?"

"Well, in India, people believe that cows are sacred."

"Oooo. Could we go there?" she asked. "I would *love* to be prayed to."

"Not now," I said.

"Some other time?"

"Sure."

"Good. What is cowhide?" she asked.

"Cowhide?" I repeated. Oh, boy. How do I answer that one? She got her robot cow to melt a bazooka because I wouldn't drink a glass of milk. What would she do when she found out we kill cows and make shoes out of them? "Cowhide is . . . a game," I said.

"A game? How is it played?"

"Well, first the cow *hides* . . . and then we try to find it."

"Oh. Like hide-and-seek?"

"Yeah, something like that."

"So what do they mean when they say suitcases are made out of cowhide?"

Oh, boy.

"Uh . . . well," I said, "it means that suitcases are sometimes made out of . . . whatever the cow *hides* in."

She nodded.

I suddenly got a terrible pain in my stomach. It was the milk. If I really hurried, I might be able to get to the Porta Potti before it was too late.

"General Bossy," I said, "I have to go to

the bathroom now. But I'll be back in a couple of minutes."

"When you return," she said, "I would like you to bring me something."

"Sure. What would you like?"

"Bring me the smartest cow in your government. I would like her to show me our cow colonies to see if they have prospered here on Earth."

"Uh, well, that might take a little time," I said.

"Take all the time you need," she said. "In the meantime we will be here, with our death rays pointed at your soldiers, and our hooves on the triggers."

"Hey," I said. "I thought you said you come in peace."

"We always *come* in peace," she said. "How we *leave* depends on what we find."

CHAPTER 4

As soon as I was done with the Porta Potti I flew straight to the White House. Director Poopington had left, but General Hurling was still in the Oval Office with the President. I told them about General Bossy's demand to meet with the smartest cow in the government.

"This could be something of a problem," said General Hurling. He turned to the

President. "Do we have any cows in government jobs?"

"Of *course* we don't have cows in government jobs, you idiot," said the President.

"OK," said General Hurling. "Hows about we just slap a skirt on a cow and stick her behind a desk to fool this General Bossy?"

"General Bossy expects our cow to talk," said the President.

"So we get a ventriloquist to talk for her," said General Hurling.

The President rolled his eyes.

"It'll work, sir," said General Hurling. "Trust me."

"Oh, Max," said the President, "I forgot to tell you. Your dad called. It seems your sister, Tiffany, got into some kind of trouble over at the Air and Space Museum."

"What kind of trouble, sir?" I asked.

"Seems she broke into one of the exhibits," said the President.

"Oh, no," I said. "Was it the space rocks exhibit?"

"That's the one," said the President. "They were going to hold her at the police station, but then she got sick. I had her sent back to Chicago on *Air Force One*. Your dad asked you to come home as soon as you can."

"What about General Bossy, sir?" I asked.

"We'll proceed with Hurling's plan and see what happens," said the President.

"Sir, you're not really going to put a skirt on a cow and get a ventriloquist to speak for her, are you?" I said.

"It's not such a bad plan," said the President.

* * *

By the time I got back to Chicago, Tiffany wasn't looking too sick. In fact, she was holding a stack of plates and was about to set the table for dinner.

"Tiffany," I said, "I hear you broke into the space rocks exhibit at the Air and Space Museum. You have personally embarrassed me in front of the President of the United States. Why the heck did you do it?"

She giggled.

"Watch," she said.

Suddenly, so fast it looked like a blur, she flipped the dinner plates out of her hands like a magician deals cards. Instead of landing in their proper places, the dishes skidded off the table, hit the floor, and shattered.

"Ooops," said Tiffany.

"Tiffany!" said my mom. "What on earth are you doing?"

Tiffany stared hard at the broken dishes on the floor. Two red beams shot out of her eyes. They hit the pieces of dishes and turned them bright orange. The dishes burst into flames and burned a hole in the floor.

"Tiffany!" said my mom. "You go to your room, young lady. And don't come out till you can set the table properly!"

Oh, no! My stupid teenage sister had gotten superpowers of her own, and she was clueless how to use them!

CHAPTER 5

I had to listen to the sounds of sobbing all through dinner. Finally, I couldn't take it any longer. I got up from the table.

"Where are you going, Max?" Dad asked.

"I can't stand to hear her crying," I said.

"Neither can I," said my mom. "Tell her she can come out and have dinner if she promises not to melt any more dishes with laser vision. I assume that's what it was, laser vision?"

"Yeah," I said, "that would be my guess."

I walked into Tiffany's room. It was dark, but Tiffany was easy to find. She was glowing a soft blue color, the same as me. She lay facedown on her bed, crying. I went and sat down next to her and patted her on the back.

"Sssshhh," I said. "Please don't cry, Tiff."

"What do *you* care?" she sobbed. "What does *anybody* in this family care? *You* handle space rocks and get superpowers, and everybody calls you a hero. *I* handle space rocks and get superpowers, and I get sent to my room."

She started sobbing again.

"Sssshhh," I said. "OK, listen to me, Tiff. I'm not thrilled you went out and got superpowers, OK? I'm really not. But you did, and you're my sister, and I care about you. So I'm going to show you how to handle these new powers of yours."

"No way," she said. "Why would you do that?"

"So you won't get sent to your room again, and so you won't destroy our apartment. You know how Dad has promised to give you driving lessons next year? Well, if you want me to, I'll give you superpower lessons."

She sat up and looked at me.

"No way! Are you making fun of me, Max?"

"No, I'm completely serious."

"But you're never here. You're either in

school or you're off on some mission for the stupid President. When would you ever have time to give me lessons?"

"Let's do your first lesson right now," I said.

"Really?"

"Come on."

We went into the dining room.

"Well, Tiffany," said my dad. "I'm glad to see you're ready to come out."

"If you promise not to melt the dishes with your laser vision, you may have some dinner," said my mom.

"I don't actually feel like having dinner right now," said Tiffany.

"If it's OK with you guys," I said, "I'd like to take Tiffany outside for a few minutes and give her some lessons in handling her superpowers."

"That's probably not such a bad idea," said my dad.

We don't live too far from Grant Park. It probably isn't the safest place to be after dark, but I figured I could handle anybody who gave us any trouble.

When we got to an open area we stopped.

"OK, Tiff," I said, "let's see what you can do." I pointed to a park bench. "See if you can lift that."

Tiffany walked over to the park bench. It had a wooden seat and back, but the rest was made out of concrete. It was planted in the ground like a tree trunk. She tried to pick it up, but after a few seconds she stopped. She was sweating and out of breath.

"Get under it, Tiff," I said. "Lift with your legs, not with your back!"

She did what I said. She tore the concrete bench out of the ground and lifted it over her head.

"Very good," I said. "Very good, Tiff. I couldn't have done it any better myself."

She looked really proud of herself.

"OK, now tell me," I said, "do you think you can fly?"

She shrugged. "I don't know," she said.

"Give it a shot," I said. "Take a good running start, then leap into the air."

She took a good running start and leaped into the air, but she only got about ten feet up and then crashed to the ground.

"Are you all right?" I said, running up to her.

"Yeah," she said, slapping off the dirt.

"OK, next time when you leap into the air, take a deep breath and flap your arms. Once you're up there, hold your arms together in front of you, like you're diving into a swimming pool."

She tried it again. This time she got about thirty feet in the air and stayed up there. She bobbed up and down, like a baby duck on a wavy lake.

"Good, Tiff! Very good!" I called. "Now let's see you turn to the right! Raise your left arm to signal for the turn!"

She turned and slammed into a tree, then crashed to the ground. I ran over to her, but she was already up when I got there, and she was laughing.

"OK, the takeoff was pretty good," I said. "But we need to work on our turns."

Just then three guys came out of the bushes. They were probably around fourteen, Tiffany's age. They had shaved heads and earrings. They wore black motorcycle jackets.

"Well, well, well. Look what we got here," said one of them. "A dork and a little babe."

"Hey, sweetheart," said another one. "Get rid of the dork and let's party."

"Get lost, buttface," I said.

All three of them burst into laughter. Then they stopped laughing and started walking slowly in my direction. I watched them come. They came up so close I could smell their breath.

"Whew!" I said. "Nice breath."

"You don't like our breath, dork?"

"No, as a matter of fact I don't," I said. "What do you use for toothpaste — dog puke?"

The biggest one took a swing at me. I caught his fist and rammed it back into his mouth pretty hard, but not as hard as I could have. He made a surprised noise, a little yelp, and sank to his knees.

The other two came at me fast. I

slammed their heads together. It sounded like two bowling pins hitting the floor. Both guys fell to the ground with a thud.

I took a little container of aspirin out of my pocket and handed it to the closest guy.

"You're all going to have pretty bad headaches for a while," I said. "Take two of these every four hours. And next time I suggest you pick on somebody younger than me. I'm eleven."

CHAPTER 6

Tiffany was pretty impressed at how I'd handled the three guys in the park. And she really appreciated the superpower lessons. It was the closest we've been since I was a little kid.

"I'm going to need two things," Tiffany announced the next morning at breakfast. "An outfit and a name. What do you like better, 'Wonder Girl' or 'The Girl Wonder'?"

"Tiffany, you are not going to be a super-hero, and that is definite," said my mom. "One superhero in the family is about all I can deal with."

"I am *so* going to be a superhero," she said. "If Max can be one, so can I. Now which name do you like better? I, myself, like 'The Girl Wonder.'"

"You're going to have to check with the League of Superheroes," I said, "but Robin is 'The Boy Wonder,' and Wonder Woman owns all other names with 'Wonder' in them."

"Lester Boogerfinger is a patent attorney," said Tiffany. "I'll ask *him* if I can be 'The Girl Wonder.'"

"You do that," I said. Lester Boogerfinger was the lawyer my parents got to defend me when everybody thought I was an international thief. Boogerfinger didn't know much about defending people, but he knew a lot about patents and trademarks and stuff.

"Now, Mom," said Tiffany, "let's talk about my outfit. You made a baseball uniform for Max, but I want something cooler. I was thinking maybe a nice jumpsuit. In leather. And I definitely want boots and a cape."

"Tiffany, I am most certainly not making you a leather outfit. Do you have any idea what leather costs? And maybe you didn't hear me. I just told you I'm not making you a uniform out of anything at all."

"But, Mom, you made one for Max. Do you like Max better?"

"Of course not, but — "

"If you won't make me a uniform, it *proves* you like Max better."

Mom rolled her eyes and sighed.

"What am I going to do with this girl?" said Mom.

"Make her an outfit," said Tiffany.

The outfit Mom made for Tiffany was pretty cool. It was a spandex jumpsuit, with a mask, high boots, and a cape, all in silver. Tiffany liked the name "Awesome Girl," and had Mom sew a black A and G on her cape. But then she decided that the word "awesome" was going to go out of style in about two more weeks, so she had Mom take it off her cape.

Lester Boogerfinger told her I was right that both names, "Wonder Girl" and "The Girl Wonder," were owned by either Robin or Wonder Woman. In fact, Boogerfinger found out that almost every name Tiffany came up with was already trademarked. He sug-

gested "A Girl Like No Other," which she hated. He also suggested "The Girl Who Flies and Stuff," and she didn't like that, either.

Tiffany called the League of Superheroes and asked to be a member. When she got off the phone she was pretty mad.

"You know what they told me?" she said. "They told me to be a member I've got to have at least three acts of heroism in which superpowers were used. Did you have three acts of heroism before you applied for membership?"

"I never applied," I said. "They read about me in the papers and offered me a membership."

"Well, isn't that *special*," she said. I think she was being sarcastic. "Max, do you know how long it's going to take me to get three acts of heroism? What can I do?"

"You could hang out under bridges and catch people who fall or jump," I said.

"But that could take forever," she said.

"Not if you pushed them."

She stuck her tongue out at me.

"Tiff, I don't think you have the true superhero spirit," I said.

Just then the phone rang. It was the President.

"Max," he said, "we need you again. Bossy wants to visit a colony of cows."

"What about General Hurling's plan of putting a skirt on a cow, sticking her behind a desk, and having a ventriloquist — "

"We've scheduled that for this afternoon at the Pentagon," said the President. "But first she wants to see a colony of cows.

She wants you to take her there this morning."

"This morning?" I said. "But I have a huge history test in about twenty minutes."

"I'll call your teacher and reschedule. You must take Bossy to a farm this morning. It's a matter of national security."

"OK," I said. "What farm should I take her to?"

"Just a minute," said the President, "I'll let you speak to General Hurling."

"Hurling here," said a gruff southern voice. "What can I do for ya?"

"General Hurling, it's Maximum Boy. The President said you had a farm for me to take General Bossy to? To see some cows? Where would you like me to take her?"

"Oh, yeah. Little farm not far from DePuke, Iowa."

"Don't you mean *Dubuque*, sir?"

"The briefing I got said it's *DePuke*, son. Anyways, here's the flying directions."

General Hurling told me exactly how to get to the farm. As soon as I hung up I put on my Maximum Boy uniform and went to the door.

"Mom, Dad, I've got another mission," I said. "I'll try not to be back late."

"Where are you going?" Tiffany asked.

"I'd love to tell you, but that's a military secret," I said.

"Oooo, Max, take me with you," said Tiffany. "Maybe I could get an act of heroism out of it."

"Tiff, I can't," I said. "Besides, you hardly know how to fly yet."

"I could learn on the way," she said.

"Yeah, right," I said.

CHAPTER 7

I offered to fly Bossy to the farm near Dubuque, but she put on a rocket pack and flew there herself. When we got there, she was the first to spot the cows. They were grazing in a field of tall grass surrounded by a barbed wire fence. Bossy was shocked.

"Are these cows being held prisoner?" she asked. "What crime have they committed?"

"I don't think they're being held prisoner, General," I said. "I think the barbed wire is to keep people from bothering them."

"And why are they naked?"

"Well, uh, I think that's because these cows are . . . nudists," I said. "This is sort of a cow nudist colony. They asked for permission to work naked, and, uh, we let them."

Bossy walked up to a cow grazing near the barbed wire fence.

"I am General Bossy, Supreme Commander of the Army of the Planet of the Cows," she said. "Why are you naked, dear?"

"Moo," said the cow.

Bossy walked up to another cow.

"What sort of job do you have here, miss?" Bossy asked.

"Moo," said the cow.

"Do they pay you well to work on this farm?"

"Moo," said the cow.

Bossy turned to me.

"These cows have poor language skills," she said.

"Maybe they're just nervous to be speaking to somebody as important as you, General," I said.

"Yes, that must be it," she said.

"I hope we'll have better luck this afternoon at the Pentagon," I said.

"If we don't," she said, "planet Earth is going to have big problems with the Planet of the Cows."

When Bossy and I arrived at the Pentagon, General Hurling himself met us. He took us to the office where the cow was supposed to be working. A lot of people stared at us as we passed. I guess they hadn't seen that many cows in space suits before.

Hurling stopped in front of an office with the name Elsie Cowper on the door. He knocked.

"Come in!" called a strange voice inside the office.

Hurling opened the door and we went in.

Behind a desk with a typewriter on it was a black-and-white cow. They had some-how gotten her to sit on an office chair and wear a skirt. Don't ask me how.

"Elsie," said Hurling, "I'd like you to meet Maximum Boy and General Bossy of the Planet of the Apes."

"The Planet of the *Cows*, you moron," said Bossy.

Hurling frowned at the "moron" part, then decided to ignore it. I think Bossy was mad about wasting time with the farm cows earlier in the day.

"Pleased to *meet* you, General Bossy," said a weird voice. The cow's lips weren't moving. The voice was clearly coming from somebody under the cow's desk.

"Elsie, tell General Bossy how important your job is here at the Pentagon," said Hurling.

"My job at the Pentagon is *very* important," said the strange voice under the desk.

"She's right," said Hurling. "Her job at the Pentagon is very important."

"Why aren't your lips moving when you speak?" Bossy asked the cow.

"Why aren't my lips moving when I speak?" the strange voice repeated. "Oh, that's because I, uh, have a cold and my lips are chapped."

Bossy glared at me.

"If this is some kind of trick," she said to the general, "I will be very angry. Believe me, you do not want to make me angry."

"No, no," said the strange voice, "this

isn't a trick, General Bossy. Honest. This is me, Elsie, talking to you."

"If it's you talking to me," said Bossy, "then why is your voice coming from under the desk?"

"Does it seem as if my voice is coming from under the desk?" said the strange voice. "Oh, how funny! That is so funny! Ha-ha-ha-ha-ha!"

While the strange voice was saying this, Elsie had started eating a whole stack of papers off the desk.

"Her voice is not coming from under the desk," said Hurling. "My information is that it's coming from Elsie herself."

"The reason my voice might *seem* like it's coming from under the desk," the strange voice continued as the cow chewed, "is, uh, that I've been learning to throw my voice. Yes, that's right. I'm training to become the first cow ventriloquist."

General Bossy walked around the desk. I followed her. Crouching underneath the desk was a man in a uniform. He looked up when he saw us.

"Oh, hi there," he said. "Hope you enjoyed the show."

Bossy turned to me.

"You told me cows had responsible jobs on farms. That was a lie. You told me cows had responsible jobs in the Pentagon. That was a lie. You told me that cowhide was a game where cows hide and others try to find them. Was that a lie as well?"

"No," said Hurling, "cowhide *is* a game. I play it back home with my kids all the time."

"Maximum Boy," said Bossy, "tell me

the truth. Is cowhide a game, or is it what suitcases are made out of?"

I looked at Hurling. I looked at Bossy. I looked at Hurling again. He was frowning and shaking his head. I looked back at Bossy.

"Pretty much the second one," I said.

"Aha!" shouted Bossy. "I thought so!"

"Are you crazy?" Hurling shouted at me. "Why are you telling her that?"

"Because!" I shouted. "I can't stand lying anymore!"

"So you admit you turn my people into suitcases?" Bossy shouted at me.

"Umm, right. And Whoppers and Happy Meals, too."

"OK!" shouted Bossy. "As of this moment, the Planet of the Cows declares war on planet Earth!"

"Fine!" I shouted. "You want a war, we'll *give* you a war! We'll kick your butts all the way back to the Milky Way!"

"Fine!" yelled Bossy. Before anyone could stop her, she charged out the door and down the hall and disappeared.

Just then something came crashing through the window into the office. It showered the room with hundreds of pieces of glass. It was Tiffany. She was wearing her new silver spandex uniform that Mom made her.

"I am Champion Girl!" she shouted. "Hero of the helpless! Defender of the weak! Who among you needs a hero?"

We all turned to stare at her.

"Oh, uh, is this a bad time?" she asked.

CHAPTER 8

"I am *so* sorry, Mr. President, sir," said Tiffany. "If I had known what was going on, I never would have crashed through the window of that office, I swear. I am *always* screwing things up at home. That's why my parents like my brother better than me. I am so so so so sorry."

"Everybody makes mistakes, Champion Girl," said the President. "Stop apologizing."

Tiffany and I were in the Oval Office with the President, General Hurling, and FBI Director Poopington.

"I wanted so much to make a good impression on everybody, and instead I started a war," said Tiffany.

"*You* didn't start a war, little lady," said Hurling. "*Maximum* Boy did."

"I admit I escalated things a little," I said. "But I didn't start a war. Whose idea was it to put a cow in a skirt, stick her behind a desk, and have a ventriloquist speak for her?"

"And that was a dadburned good idea!" shouted Hurling.

"People! People!" said the President. "Stop this arguing! We've got a situation here. We have an interplanetary war on our hands."

"Not an interplanetary war," said General Hurling. "A stupid barnyard animal in a flying barn had a hissy fit. Big deal. She'll calm down by nightfall and this will all blow over."

A secretary ran in and handed the President a message. He read it and frowned.

"People, I have some disturbing news," he said. "At this moment, flying barns have surrounded the farm outside Cedar Rapids where Bossy's vehicle is parked. Tanks of the Iowa National Guard have attempted to attack the flying barns. But the cows spread melted butter all over and the tanks are sliding out of control. The cows have hit National Guardsmen with stinky cheese gas spray and cow pies. People, the war has just begun, and already we are losing."

"Mr. President," said Director Poopington, "this is a critical hour in our nation's history. It is a time for leadership. It is a time for statesmanship. What do you think we should tell the American people about the invaders from outer space?"

"Tell them the flying barns are weather balloons and hubcaps that fell off airplanes," said Hurling. "It's worked before, it'll work again."

"But flying barns don't *look* like weather balloons or hubcaps," I said.

"Neither do UFO's," said Hurling.

"So you want to tell them that weather balloons have surrounded a farm in Iowa?" I said.

"They'll buy it," said Hurling. "They always do."

"Maximum Boy," said the President, "your country needs you in Iowa."

"What about me?" asked Tiffany. "I'm a superhero now, too."

"Are you a member of the League of Superheroes, Champion Girl?" asked the President.

"Not exactly," said Tiffany. "Listen, do you *like* the name 'Champion Girl'? Because I'm starting to think it's not so great anymore. What about 'Thunder Girl'? Do you like that better? Or maybe 'Mega Girl'?"

"If you're not a member of the League of Superheroes," said the President, "I don't think I'm allowed to send you out on any missions."

"Why not?" said Tiffany. "You think I'd get hurt? I wouldn't get hurt. I've got superpowers. You want to see? Look."

She reached for a heavy marble pedestal with a bust of George Washington on it. She lifted the pedestal over her head with one hand. Washington's bust slid off the pedestal and landed on her foot. Her eyes bugged out.

"OK," she said, "that really hurt. I admit it. But it doesn't mean I have no super-powers. Watch *this*."

She bent down, grabbed one leg of the President's desk, and lifted it over her head.

"Not bad," said the President.

She bent down, grabbed General Hurling by one ankle, and lifted him over her head.

"Put me down," said Hurling.

She put Hurling down. Then she stared hard at a metal wastebasket by the side of the desk. Two beams of red light shot out of her eyes and hit the wastebasket. The wastebasket turned bright orange and

melted, burning a hole in the Oval Office floor.

"OK," said the President, "no more demonstrations. I believe you've got super-powers. If you really want to serve your country, you may go with Maximum Boy to Iowa."

"All right!" said Tiffany and gave the President a high five.

CHAPTER 9

Because Tiffany had flown to Washington by herself, I let her fly with me to Iowa. She was still pretty wobbly in the air. She almost flew smack into the top of the Washington Monument. Then she lost altitude and would have fallen into the Potomac River if I hadn't grabbed her.

"If this is how you fly," I said, "how'd

you ever make it from Chicago to Washington without killing yourself?"

We were flying at our cruising altitude of a thousand feet, zooming along just below a cloud bank.

"Well, Max," she said, "I didn't exactly fly the whole way."

"What do you mean?"

"OK, I jumped into the air in Chicago, right? But when I got over Gary, Indiana, I got scared by an American Airlines plane that got too close to me. So I landed and took a train to Pittsburgh. I got into the air again and was OK till Baltimore, where I was attacked by a gang of seagulls. So I landed again and hitchhiked to Washington."

"When we get back home," I said, "you need to have a few more lessons."

We arrived over the farm where Bossy

had her UFO. We looked down. Far below us lay the tanks and soldiers. From a thousand feet up, their arrangement looked like a target at a shooting gallery. In the middle was Bossy's UFO. Surrounding her UFO was a ring of maybe 200 National Guardsmen with tanks and bazookas. Surrounding the National Guard was another ring of flying-barn UFO's.

There was some kind of fighting going on down there, but we were too high up to see what was going on. We drifted lower.

Now we could see. The soldiers were shooting at the flying barns, but they weren't doing any damage. The flying barns were shooting stinky cheese bombs and cow pies at the soldiers. Bork, the robot cow, was clanking slowly from tank to tank, flattening them like pizza boxes. Bork moved so slowly, the soldiers in the tanks had plenty of time to escape.

"Max, look out!" shouted Tiffany.

Suddenly, something whizzed past my head. I whirled around. It was a cow in a space suit with a rocket pack. Bossy! She turned and came at me again. She was holding a nasty-looking pitchfork, the kind used to pick up hay on farms.

"You're toast, Earth boy!" she screamed as she whooshed toward me.

I dodged at the last minute. The sharp prongs of the steel pitchfork missed me by maybe an inch.

"Hey, you stupid cow!" I shouted. "Why are you trying to kill me?"

She whirled and came at me again.

"Because you make Whoppers out of my people!" she screamed.

"Not me!" I shouted. "I'm not the one who does that! I'm the one who was honest enough to tell you the truth! Remember?"

Whoosh! This time, Bossy and her pitchfork missed me by *half* an inch.

"You're as guilty as those who make the patties!" she screamed. "Now, I'm going to make a patty out of *you*!"

"You wouldn't like the taste!" I shouted as she came at me again. "Humans taste awful!"

"No, you're very tasty!" she screamed. "On our planet you're a delicacy!"

Whoosh! She missed me a third time.

"What?" shouted Tiffany. "You have humans on the Planet of the Cows?"

"When we left cows on planet Earth, we brought back herds of humans! You people are good for nothing but food! People Patties with cheese are my favorite!"

"You eat people?!" I shouted. "OK, now I'm *really* mad!"

"Max, look out!" Tiffany called.

Something hit me in the shoulder and whizzed past. Another cow in a space suit, carrying a pitchfork! I glanced at my shoulder. It was trickling blood. I turned around. The sky was filthy with flying cows! And they were all carrying steel pitchforks!

"Tiff, I'm going to need your help!" I called. "You take all the cows near you, I'll take all those near me! And use your laser!"

"Right!" Tiffany called back.

We went into action.

A cow came toward me. I focused my laser vision on her pitchfork. It went orange. The steel prongs melted. The cow seemed confused. I punched her hard in the head. Her helmet shattered, and the cow went into a screaming nosedive.

Another cow charged me. I did the same to her.

"How you doing, Tiff?" I called.

"Great!" she called back.

She'd seen what I was doing and was now doing the same. Cows were dropping like flies on all sides of us. We were definitely thinning the herd.

"Hey, Max!" she called out. "We must be cowboys!"

"Why?"

"Because we're punching cattle!" she said, whooping with laughter.

I punched out two cows at once. They dropped like lead weights.

"I don't get it!" I said.

"It's a joke, Max! Cowboys are called cowpunchers!"

"Oh!" I said.

I looked down. Far below us, the soldiers were taking advantage of our work in the air. They rushed over to each downed cow and tied it up. I couldn't figure out where all the cows were coming from. Maybe from the flying barns?

Looking down was a mistake. Two cows charged me and almost finished me off. I went into maximum speed. I punched both of them out of the sky. Tiffany was doing well, too. Now there were only six cows left. Now four. Now two. Now one. The boss. General Bossy herself.

"General Bossy!" I shouted. "Your army is finished! I don't want to hurt you! Surrender now!"

"Eat cow pies, Earth boy!" General Bossy screamed.

That got me even madder. Far below me, the soldiers had corralled all the cows except for Bork, the robot cow. Bork was busily flattening another tank. She didn't seem to know or care that soldiers on all sides of her were now setting the flying barns on fire.

I swooped down, landed, grabbed Bork underneath by her steel udders, and flew straight up again. Bossy saw me coming and realized too late what I was up to.

"Noooooo!" she screamed as I smashed into her with the giant steel cow.

Pieces of steel flew in all directions. General Bossy sailed a hundred feet higher before going into her final nosedive.

CHAPTER 10

"Congratulations, Max," said the President, getting up from behind his desk in the Oval Office. "With only a little help from the U.S. Air Force and the National Guard, you almost single-handedly defeated the invaders from the Planet of the Cows."

"Thank you, sir," I said, "but it wasn't only me. I never could have done it without the help of my sister, Tiffany. We did it together."

"Really, Max?" said Tiffany. I thought I saw tears in her eyes.

"Absolutely," I answered.

"Very well, then," said the President. "I hereby congratulate the two of you for saving this planet from a fearsome enemy. The people of America owe Maximum Boy and Champion Girl a giant debt of gratitude."

"Thank you, sir," I said.

"Thank you, Mr. President," said Tiffany.

"Unfortunately," said the President, "the people of America must never learn what you two kids did today in Iowa."

"Why not, sir?" I asked.

"Because. Can you imagine the reaction if we said we were nearly conquered by

a hostile army of extraterrestrial cows? There'd be panic in the streets. No, no, we could never permit that. It should be enough to know that your President is undyingly grateful. And now, if you don't mind, I see I have a call on my private line."

Tiffany and I left the Oval Office and walked out of the White House. The sun was just setting in the west. It was a beautiful evening.

"Max, I've been thinking," said Tiffany. "I don't really like the name 'Champion Girl' after all. Would you mind very much if I called myself 'Maximum Girl'?"

"Not at all," I said. "In fact, I'd be honored."

**Check out this sneak
preview from the next
nail-biting Maximum Boy Adventure!**

MAXIMUM GIRL UNMASKED

"Guess what! I'm going to be on, like, the front page of our school newspaper!"

"That's lovely, Tiffany," said my mother. "What did you do?"

"I won the high jump in gym."

"How high did you jump?" I asked. I was beginning to get a really bad feeling.

"Twenty-one feet," she said proudly. "It was so *cool*."

"Twenty-one feet!" I said. "Are you *crazy*?"

"What do you mean?"

"Tiffany, no ordinary human being can high-jump twenty-one feet," I said. "By showing off and using your superpowers, you're going to blow our secret identities."

"Oh, relax, Max," said Tiffany. "Don't get your undies in a knot. Nobody outside Bosco High is ever going to *hear* about this. Besides, the coach wants me on the track team now, and I'm suddenly popular in my school for, like, the first time in *history*. I've even been invited to a big sleepover party this weekend. So it's worth it."

"It is not!"

"Is so!"

"Is not!"

"Is so!"

"Mom, is it OK with you that Tiffany has blown our secret identities and exposed you and Dad to life-threatening danger?"

"Well, Tiffany," said my mom, "Max does have a point. I mean, if the media find out you're Maximum Girl, then . . ."

"Then *what*?" said Tiffany.

"Then supervillains could kidnap Mom and Dad," I said. "And use them to force us to stop battling the forces of evil. But you're so selfish, all you could think of was showing off for your stupid friends."

"That is so *untrue*," said Tiffany. "I don't even *have* any friends. I was showing off for, like, total *strangers*."

THE KID CRUSADER WITH A CURFEW.

by DAN GREENBURG

■ **SCHOLASTIC**

MB 1101